CINDERELLA
BIGFOOT

by Mike Thaler
Illustrated by Jared Lee

SCHOLASTIC INC.
New York Toronto London Auckland Sydney

For Di,
whose bright ideas
are editorial lightbulbs!
—M.T.

To Jana and Jennifer,
Daughters. Friends. Glowbugs.
—J.L.

ISBN 0-590-89826-4

Text copyright © 1997 by Mike Thaler.
Illustrations copyright © 1997 by Jared D. Lee Studio, Inc.
All rights reserved. Published by Scholastic Inc.
HAPPILY EVER LAUGHTER is a trademark of Mike Thaler.
Library of Congress Catalog Card Number: 96-68251.
12 11 10 9 8 7 6 5 4 3 2 1   7 8 9/9 0 1 2/0
Printed in the U.S.A.
First Scholastic printing, March 1997   24

Once upon a time, about 8:30,
in the Land of Make Believe,
there lived a girl named Cinderella.

Now, there were a lot of funny-looking people in the Land of Make Believe, but Cinderella was the funniest.

Her most outstanding feature was her big feet.
When she stood up, she looked like a seaplane.

Cinderella lived with her beautiful stepmother
and her three beautiful stepsisters, Weeny, Whiny, and Moe.
She also had a beautiful stepcat,
a stepdog,
and a stepladder.

The size of Cinderella's feet caused her many problems.
She bounced off the ceiling in ballet class,
she always lost at hopscotch,
and she had to buy a sock for every toe.

However, the worst problem for everyone else
was that when Cinderella's bunions bothered her,
she'd take off her shoes and leave them around town.
The giant, smelly shoes would block doorways,
stop traffic, and take up four parking spaces at the mall.

So, when the King and Queen of the Land of Make Believe
gave a dance party,
they naturally didn't invite Cinderella.

On the evening of the ball,
the stepsisters stepped into
their party dresses.
"Isn't it exciting!" said Weeny.
"Tonight the Prince will choose a bride," said Whiny.
"I hope it's one of us," chirped Moe.

But Cinderella wasn't much interested.
She was trying to remember where she had left her other sneaker.
Soon it was time to leave for the ball.
"Good-bye-ee," twittered Cinderella's stepmother.
"Good-bye-ee," chattered Weeny, Whiny, and Moe.

As soon as they were gone,
Cinderella put her feet up
and turned on her favorite TV show,
Lifestyles of the Royal and Famous.

Suddenly, a cow wearing a blond wig and a pink tutu
appeared on top of the TV.
"Would you please move your tail?" asked Cinderella.
"You're blocking the screen."
"I'm Elsie, your Dairy Godmother," replied the cow.
"And I'm here to send you to the ball."
"I wasn't invited," said Cinderella.

The cow waved her golden wand.
Just then, an invitation dropped through the mail slot.

"I don't have a thing to wear," whined Cinderella.
Elsie waved her golden wand again.
Cinderella was suddenly wearing a glamorous, glittering gown.

"I can't find my other sneaker," sniveled Cinderella.
The cow twirled her wand.
On Cinderella's feet sparkled two glass sneakers.

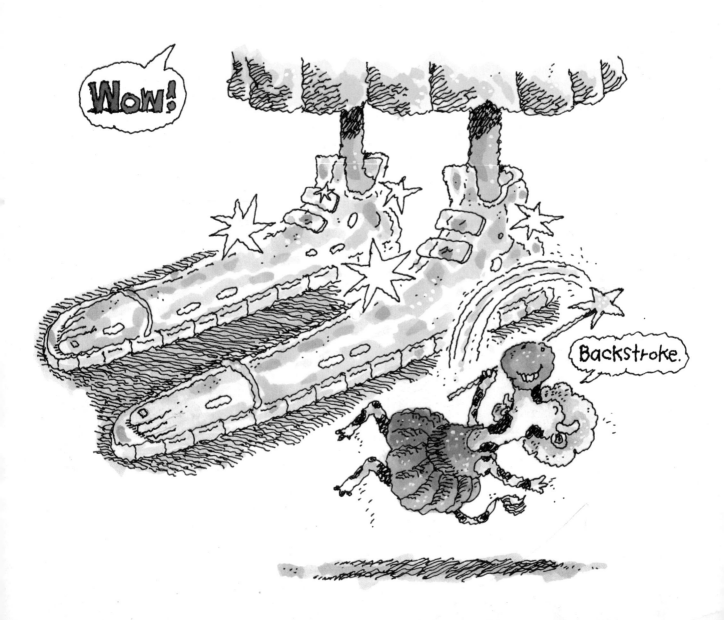

"I don't have a carriage," moaned Cinderella.
"Take the bus," said her Dairy Godmother,
handing Cinderella some change.
"Thank you, Dairy Godmother," said Cinderella.
She turned to leave.

"One more thing," said the cow.
"You have to be back before the clock strikes twelve."
"Sure, sure," said Cinderella. "Bye."

When Cinderella arrived at the ball,
everyone pointed and said,
"Who's that funny-looking girl?"

Prince Smeldred, who was quite funny looking himself,
raised his head from the punch bowl and sputtered,
"Who's the doll! Wanna dance?"

"Let's trip the light fantastic, big boy," said Cinderella, twirling.

"Ouch!" said Smeldred. "You stepped on my foot!"
The two began to dance.
"Ouch!
Ouch!
Ouch! Maybe we'd better sit this one out," howled Smeldred,
hopping up and down.
Just then the clock struck twelve.
(Time goes fast when you're having a ball.)

"I have to go," shrieked Cinderella.
"But who are you?" cried Smeldred, rubbing his feet.
"I'm late!" she replied.
"That's a funny name," said Smeldred, who wasn't too swift.
"What's your address? What's your phone number?
What's your sign?"
But Cinderella was gone.

She'd left behind one glass sneaker —
size 87, triple A — that blocked the doorway,
so everyone had to leave through the back door.

"I'm going to find that girl," vowed Smeldred.
Using a "toe" truck, he hauled the sneaker to
every maiden in the kingdom.
Each girl would put in one foot,
then two feet,
then both hands.

Finally, Smeldred arrived at Cinderella's house.
Weeny sat in the sneaker.
"It fits!" she shrieked.
"Next," said Smeldred.

Then Whiny and Moe stood in the sneaker together.
"It fits!" they shouted.
"Next!" sighed Smeldred, feeling a little discouraged.

Just then, Cinderella lumbered into the room.
"Oh, there's my other sneaker!" she cried, and slipped it on.
Everyone stared at Cinderella's foot.
"It fits!" they gasped.
"Will you marry me?" said Smeldred, throwing himself at her feet.
"Only if you'll marry *me*," replied Cinderella.
The Prince grabbed a doughnut and put it on her finger.
Then they rushed out the door to live happily ever after.

"Well, at least the Prince will be our stepbrother-in-law,"
cried Weeny, Whiny, and Moe.
"Yeah, but it's going to be hard to fill Cinderella's shoes,"
sighed their mom.

Just then, Elsie appeared on top of the refrigerator.
"The shoe must go on," she uttered with a wink,
and poured them each a glass of milk.